MY FAVORITE DREAM

by Judi Dunn & Elliot Dunn

ILLUSTRATED BY AJ VANDIS

INDIE OWL PRESS KIDS

INDIE OWL PRESS KIDS
Orlando, FL 32839

info@indieowlpress.com
IndieOwlPress.com

MY FAVORITE DREAM

Illustrated by A.J. Vandis
Book Design by NightOwlFreelance.com

ISBN-13: 978-1-949193-38-1

For Jules Bodhi Dunn

One Day, upon a time, Oma went on a picnic with Jason, Sveta, and Elliot...

They went to their favorite field and spread out a big blanket under a large Oak tree.

The ground was soft and dry. The tree gave them shade. They all loved the sound of the wind in the leaves and the birds in the tree.

Such a magical place!

Mama had packed a delicious lunch. They had berries, melon, chips, and sandwiches. The sandwiches were so creamy, and the bread was extra delicious.

They had extra food, though! Jason, Sveta, and Elliot said they wished Elliot had a little brother to enjoy eating lunch with. They talked all afternoon about how fun it would be for Elliot to have a brother.

"We have so much love to share!" Oma said.

After eating their dessert of coconut date balls, they all felt very tired.

Sveta said, "Hey, let's all take a nap."

The tree shaded their eyes; the ground was soft, and the breeze was perfect. As they lay together on the ground, they all made the same wish: "We wish for a baby brother."
Feeling love all around them, they all snuggled together and fell asleep.

Next thing Oma and Elliot knew, they were wide awake! They saw Jason and Sveta (Dad and Mom) still sleeping.

Elliot said, "Hey, Oma, look, the rainbow's end is right by our blanket!"

Elliot and Oma got up off the blanket while Mom and Dad slept. Elliot stood at the very end of the rainbow. Oma could see sparkles all around Elliot's body and feet.

Quickly, Oma got up and stood in a puddle of rainbows with Elliot. They felt a tingle of energy. Then, POP! They felt light. It was magical, like they could fly.

Looking up at the rainbow, there were unicorns with rainbow manes dancing and prancing in the sky. One special unicorn slid down to Elliot and Oma.

Oma picked up Elliot, and they hopped on the unicorn's back. Up Up and away! Oma and Elliot rode over the rainbow.

Elliot said, "Oma, where are we going?"

All of a sudden, the unicorn turned her head around and spoke. She said, "We are going to the land of rainbows, of course!"

"Wow," said Elliot, that's where I came from!

"Yes," said the unicorn. "The land of rainbows is a pure and magical place."

More unicorns came and led the way through prisms over the rainbow.

A few minutes went by, and they could see a rainbow-colored land below.

Oma and Elliot flew down to the end of the rainbow, landing in a field of multicolored flowers.

The whole place smelled beautiful and glistened with light.

The unicorn started eating the flowers! She said the rainbow flowers made her mane extra colorful.

Elliot and Oma decided to explore.

"How will we get back to Daddy and Momma?" asked Elliot.

"Don't worry," said the unicorn, the rainbow magic will always take you where you need to go!"

Elliot and Oma felt so happy and began exploring.

Elliot said, "Look at all those bigger flowers over there! They seem to have faces!

Oma, of course, was encouraged to go check it out. "Let's go see," she said.

Walking through a field of small flowers, they came to the big ones.

The flowers were alive.

Not like regular flowers, these spoke!

They all said, "Pick me, pick me!"

Looking closely, Oma and Elliot saw they were not flowers at all! They were small babies! Real Babies!

One stood out from the rest. It was a purple boy flower with big brown eyes and a loving smile.

"I pick you," Elliot said.

Just then, the branches of the flower turned into arms with tiny little hands.

Little baby flower reached out to Elliot. He said, "Pick me, pick me!"

So Elliot did. He picked up the baby boy and carried him back through the small flowers to the field where the unicorn was grazing.

"Oh, good, you found him," said the lovely unicorn! "Time to go!"

Oma took Baby Flower from Elliot's hands and wrapped him tightly to her chest.

"We are ready to go," said Elliot.

Lady Unicorn beckoned them to hop back up on her back, and back over the rainbow they flew.

Elliot was sitting on the front of the unicorn, holding her mane.

Oma sat right behind Elliot with Baby Flower strapped to her chest and her arms around Elliot's body.

"Wait until Momma and Daddy see our Baby Flower!" said Elliot.

Going back over the rainbow was even more magical than the first trip to the land of rainbows.

The energy was tingling all over their bodies.

There were bubbles of rainbows following them in the air.

They were at the top of the rainbow and could not see the ground at either end.

They could just feel warm love.

Within a few minutes they were gliding down, down, down. It was so relaxing that they both fell asleep right there on the back of a unicorn.

The next thing they knew, they were back on the blanket with Sveta and Jason, who were still sleeping.

Elliot and Oma were lying there, just waking up on the ground. Oma said, "Where's the unicorn? Was it a dream?"

Elliot said, "No, Oma, we went to the land of rainbows!" We both had the same dream! It has to be real!"

"But where is Baby Flower?" asked Oma.

Just then, Elliot began to cry. Oma started crying too.

Mommy and Daddy woke up. "What's wrong, sweetheart?" said Mommy.

Elliot explained, "When we went to sleep, we wished and prayed for a baby brother. We went to the land of rainbows and found a sweet baby with big brown eyes and a loving smile, and he is gone!"

Sveta said, "You did! You brought him to us!"

"But how?" asked Elliot.

"Magically, he is now growing in my belly!" said Mama.

They all put their hands on Svetas' belly. Just then, Baby Flower pushed his hand against the skin of Momma's belly. They all gave him a high five.

Perfect little boy was going to be the baby brother! He picked out Elliot! Elliot had held his hand in the magical land, and Oma had held him tightly as they traveled back from the land of rainbows where magic and wishes come from.

A few months later, baby brother was born!

He looked just like the flower, with love in his eyes and a big smile.

They were all happy and grateful for their family. Momma and Daddy named the beautiful baby Jules, which stands for adventure with confidence and love.

Now Jules is getting bigger every day. He is more fun all the time! With great ideas, Jules loves adventures and always has confidence and love in his heart.

Everyone loves Jules. He is their favorite dream come true.

ABOUT THE AUTHOR

Judi Dunn is a spiritual woman who finds ways to express her love through crafting children's books. She is a meditation leader with an open heart, cherishing her family. She celebrates that love through her line of Rainbow Books. This story was written for Jules Dunn with help from his big brother Elliot Dunn. Elliot knows about the land of rainbows from his own storybook, *Elliot's Chakras*. In this book, Elliot and Oma find baby Jules in the land of rainbows.

www.ingramcontent.com/pod-product-compliance
Lightning Source LLC
Chambersburg PA
CBHW041033170626

46815CB00005B/298